Pooleville Pete

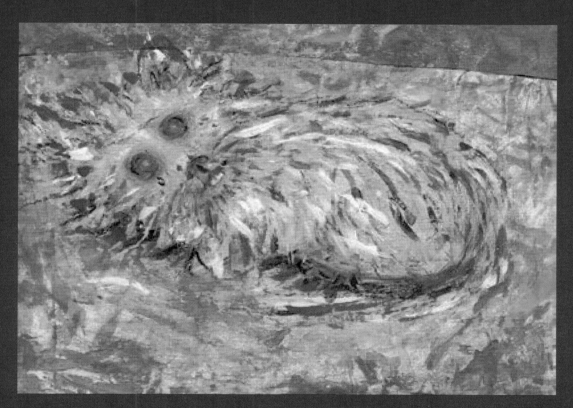

Written by Kathleen Mancuso
Illustrated by Monica Gartler

Amelia Press

Printed in the United States of America

Kathleen Mancuso/ Monica Gartler

Pooleville Pete/Mancuso and Gartler- 1st Edition

ISBN: 978-0-9996208-0-9

1. Pooleville Pete. 2. Children's Book. 3. Illustrations. 4. Animals.
5. Mancuso and Gartler

Amelia Press
is an imprint of NFB
<<<>>>
NFB Publishing/Amelia Press
119 Dorchester Road
Buffalo, New York 14213
For more information visit
nfbpublishing.com

To Lucia, Oliver, Holly and Chris

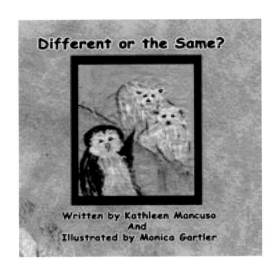

Different or the Same?

Written by Kathleen Mancuso
And
Illustrated by Monica Gartler

Kathleen & Monica's first book
Different or the Same?

And Coming Soon:
Two More Books Featuring Molly

Molly's Surprise
&
Greyhounds Like Walks Too!

Pooleville Pete is a groundhog. He is eight years old. Every February second for his entire life, the townspeople would wake him up out of a deep sleep. They would pull him out of his hole. Sometimes the sun would be in his face.

Every February second Pete would cry because he was still so tired. He didn't understand why they woke him up and took him out of his warm, cozy home.

Molly is a little girl. She is eight years old too! She is a second grader at Collinswood Parkway Elementary School. Molly had always heard about Pooleville Pete. She heard that every February 2nd if Pete saw his shadow there would be six more weeks of winter weather. If he didn't see his shadow, there would be early spring weather.

This year would be very special for Molly. She was going with her dad on Groundhog Day to see Pooleville Pete.

On Febuary 1st, Molly said to her dad, "I can't wait until tomorrow when I finally get to see Pete!"

"Yes, we will have so much fun," said her dad.

It was the big day. Groundhog Day! Molly dressed in her warm clothes. She and her dad were holding hands and gathered around Pete's home. All of the townspeople were there. Then everyone clapped and Dave, the bakery owner, at 9:00am sharp, pulled the sleeping Pete out of his hole.

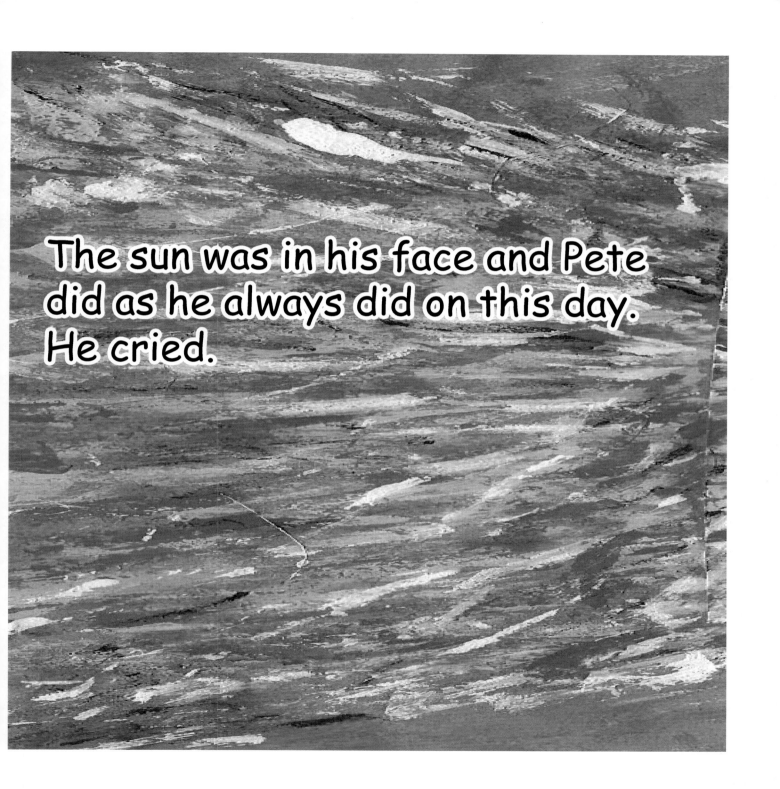

The sun was in his face and Pete did as he always did on this day. He cried.

Molly had a smile on her face at first. Then she saw that poor Pete was crying. Suddenly her smile was gone and she also began to cry. Her dad said, "What's wrong honey?"

Molly replied, "Pete is crying and it is so sad!"

Molly's dad took her home. She told her mom and everyone she could that it was terrible when she saw Pete cry. Molly told her teachers and her friends about her feelings. She decided to do something about the unfair Groundhog Day that she had seen.

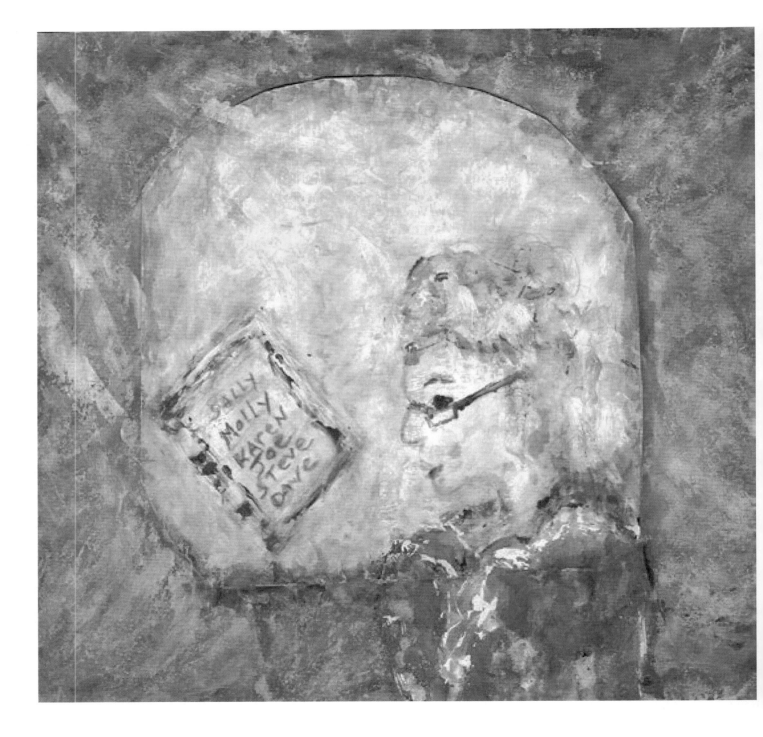

Molly asked her dad when the townspeople would have a meeting. He told her it would be in the summer.

Mrs. Spoth, Molly's teacher said, "Why don't you get a petition?"

"What's a petition?" Molly asked.

"It's a list of people who sign a paper to say they don't like the way something is done," said Mrs. Spoth.

"Yes," said Molly. "I will do that!" Molly got everyone she knew to sign her petition.

Then Molly and her dad went to the meeting in the summer. At first the townspeople said that Molly was just being silly. Then she showed them all of the people that signed her petition.

Dave the baker said, "But what will we do on February 2nd if we don't wake up Pete?"

Molly had an idea. She said, "We will just wait until he wakes up and comes out of his hole. Then that is when the nice spring weather will begin!" The townspeople took a vote. Molly's idea won!

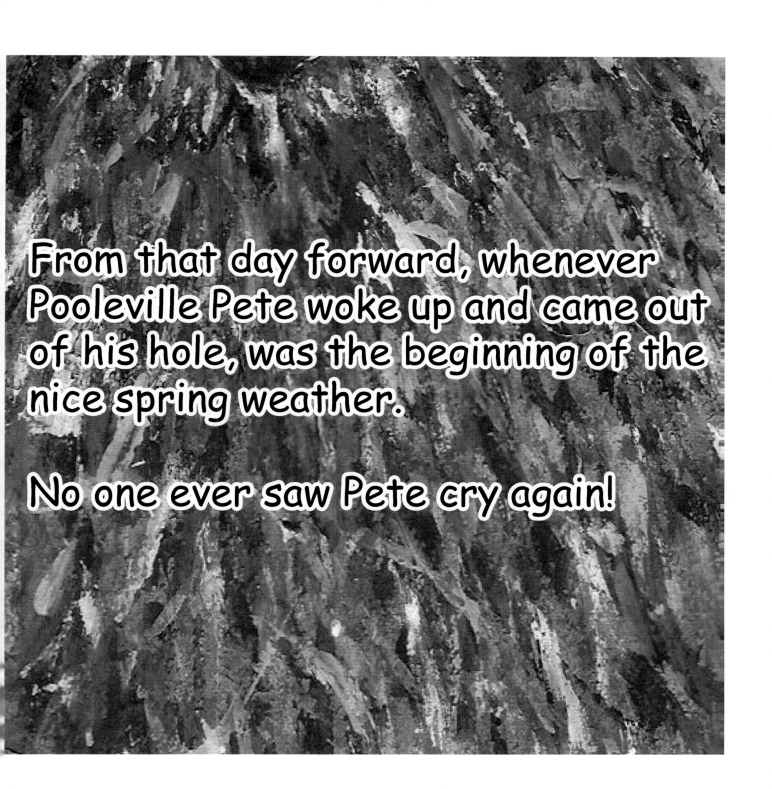

From that day forward, whenever Pooleville Pete woke up and came out of his hole, was the beginning of the nice spring weather.

No one ever saw Pete cry again!

Together on the path of knowledge

Kathleen Mancuso
Katk47@gmail.com

Monica Gartler
Monicagartler@yahoo.com

Pooleville Pete is the second book collaboration between cousins Kathleen and Monica.

Kathleen lives in Western New York where she's been very busy working on several book projects as well as attending book events for their first book, *Different or the Same?*

Monica moved to Los Angeles where she is an actress and has worked in several television series. She is an award winning artist and has published a novel, *Beyond the Horizon*.

Made in the USA
Middletown, DE
11 December 2017